A JUST ONE MORE BOOK
Just For You

All My Toys
Are On the Floor

by Mary Blocksma

Illustrated by Sandra Cox Kalthoff

Developed by The Hampton-Brown Company, Inc.

CHILDRENS PRESS ®

CHICAGO

Word List

Give children books they can read by themselves, and they'll always ask for JUST ONE MORE. This book is written with 76 of the most basic words in our language, all repeated in an appealing rhythm and rhyme.

a	floor	noise	take
all		noisy	tap
and	get	now	tell
are			that
around	had	of	the
as	hard	off	them
at	heard	on	then
away	hee	once	thing
	how	one	think
bear		opened	to
began	I('ll)		today
boom	in	picked	toys
but	it	pig	
		plane	up
closet	just	put	
clown			were
could	laughed	room	why
course	let		worked
		said	
dancing	me	say	you
dolls	more	shut	
door	my	so	zing
		still	zoom
fell	nap	stop	

Library of Congress Cataloging-in-Publication Data

Blocksma, Mary.
    All my toys are on the floor.

    (A Just one more book just for you)
    Summary: A little girl explains why her toys
are in a big mess all over her bedroom floor.
    [1.   Stories in rhyme.   2.   Toys—Fiction]
I.   Kalthoff, Sandra Cox, ill.   II.   Title.   III.   Series.
PZ8.3.B5983Wi   1986   [E]   85-27000
ISBN 0-516-01579-6   AACR2

My toys were on the floor today.

Of course, I put them all away.

I worked so hard, I had to say,
"I think I'll take a nap today."

But just as I began to nap,
my dancing dolls began to **tap.**

Tap-a-tap-a-tap-a-tap!

Now how could I take a nap?

8

Then the bear
began to **zoom,**
zoom-a-zoom
around the room.

Zoom-a-zoom, tap-a-tap!
Now how could I take a nap?

Then the clown laughed,
"Hee-hee-hee!"
It laughed and laughed
and laughed at me.

Hee-hee-hee, a-zoom-a-tap!
Now how could I take a nap?

Then the pig
began to **boom,**
boom-a-boom
around the room.

Boom-a-boom, zoom, hee, tap!
Now how could I take a nap?

Then the plane
began to **zing,**
zing-a-zing-a-zing-a-zing.

Zing-a-zoom, boom, hee, tap!
Now how could I take a nap?

ZING-A-ZING, HEE-HEE, ZOOM!

TAP-A-TAP, ZING-ZING, BOOM!

How could I nap in all that noise?
I had to stop my noisy toys!

"Stop!" I said.

"Now stop that noise!

Get in the closet, noisy toys!"

I picked the toys up off the floor.
I put them in,
and SHUT THE DOOR!

But then I heard a **zing-a-zing!**
I had to get JUST ONE MORE thing!

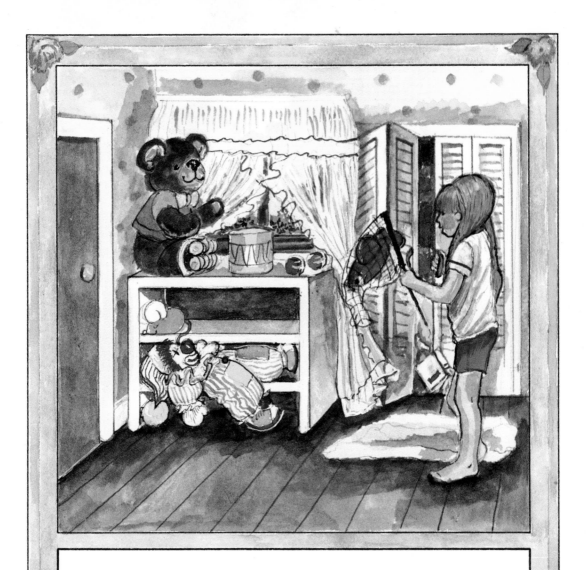

I had to put in JUST ONE MORE.
And so I opened up the door....

Then all my toys...

. . . fell on the floor!

Why are my toys STILL on the floor?

Let me tell you JUST ONCE MORE....